THE WORLD OF CHINESE MAGAZINE

《汉语世界》杂志社编

ON THE CHINESE ROAD

Stefan Schomann

坐着火车看中国

〔德〕史岱帆·舒曼

商务印书馆
SINCE 1897 The Commercial Press

2011, Beijing

ABOUT THE AUTHOR:
Stefan Schomann, born in 1962, has been freelancing as a journalist since 1988, writing for *GEO, Stern* magazine, *DIE ZEIT, Frankfurter Rundschau* and *National Geographic*. He lives in Berlin and visits China regularly. He recently published a book about the Jewish emigration to Shanghai during World War II.

Publisher: Yu Dianli

Production Supervisor: Zhou Hongbo

Mastermind / Chief Editor: Cao Quan

Art director / Designer: Yuke Wang

Executive Editors: Wen Xuechun, He Hongtao, Huang Yuanjing

Proofreaders: Yu Libin, Zhao Yuhong

Special thanks to:

Zhu Xiaojian, H.R.Lan (USA), David N. Tool (USA), Li Bing,

Cui Yonghua, Andy Deemer (USA), Jonathan Heeter (USA),

Robert Lewis Livingston (USA), Nicholas Richards (Canada),

Tian Wenzhu, Zhao Zhankun, Ma Shirui

CHAPTERS

BEIJING MOMENTS

Běijīng Shùnjiān

北京瞬间

For a few weeks in August 2008, the whole world was focused on Beijing. The Olympic Games left their mark on China's capital, but now, life goes on as usual. German writer Stefan Schomann recently spent a few months in Beijing. Here are some of his impressions of a drastically changing city.

The unique structure of the Olympic stadium continues to arouse a lot of curiosity and admiration. It immediately became a major tourist attraction.

Old and new? In fact, both the pavilion and the apartment buildings are new. The location is old and historic. There used to be a bell temple here.

For forty years now, Mr. Liu has been repairing bicycles in a *hutong* in southern Beijing.

The high-speed train between Beijing South Station and Tianjin is currently the fastest regular passenger train in the world. It reaches 350 km/h.

That's a classic dish: Peking Duck. Most people find it irresistible – be they Chinese or foreign.

"Lan Club" is one of the craziest designer bars and restaurants in the city.

It always amazes me to see the abundance of fresh fish in the city. I have never had a bad experience with fish and seafood in China.

Water is a key resource for every city, both practically and aesthetically. Beijing could make better use of this simple treasure. It immediately changes and enriches the urban landscape.

This is the main building of the Communication University of China (CUC), the most important higher learning institution for media and TV in the whole country. When visiting Beijing, I usually live here on campus.

Taking the subway is always an experience. Shortly before the Olympics, several new lines were opened; another one will start to operate soon.

What a sweet team! I took this picture from a taxi – a quick snapshot, a funny moment in the life of the city.

A spectacular new shopping center has been opened in Chaoyang District. Special films are projected on the roof of the atrium.

Qianmen Dajie, an old commercial street, has just reopened after massive reconstruction. It recalls the Beijing of the '20s and '30s.

Having a rest. Despite Beijing's fast pace, its people have kept a special talent for relaxing.

AN ILLUSTRATIVE GLIMPSE

Datong and Ningbo were once China's cultural and trade capitals, respectively

Shuāngchéng Tújì

双城图记

Two cities of great historical significance provide insight into China's past, present and future.

Coffee tables on a terrace along the Yong Jiang. Elements of Europe are scattered throughout the city, this being one of the more breathtaking scenes.

NINGBO 宁波

Long before Shanghai, Ningbo was known as the most important harbor on China's East Coast. Ships came from the neighboring countries of Korea and Japan, as well as distant lands surrounding the Arabian Sea, to conduct trade with Ningbo natives. Moving forward in time to the 16th century, it was not uncommon to see early European traders from Portugal or Holland pull onto the city's bustling blue shores. Today, Ningbo's fame has since faded, but its beauty remains intact.

The gate to Xikou, an old town about 60 kilometers south of Ningbo. The location has proven itself to be a popular destination amongst tourists, thanks largely in part to its charming mountain environment.

Ningbo is a city of two rivers: the Yao Jiang (姚江 Yáo Jiāng) and the Fenghua Jiang (奉化江 Fènghuà Jiāng).

Ningbo's historic district's recent redevelopment has resulted in a post-modern synthesis of what once was and what now is.

After the Opium Wars, Portuguese and English imperial powers from Europe established their architectural presence along the banks of the Yong Jiang. The resulting boulevard was referred to as the Bund, a word of Indian origin.

This romantic pavilion, covered with a pagoda roof, overlooks Qianzhang (千丈 Qiānzhàng) Rock Waterfall.

A pioneer of international cooperation, Nottingham University from the U.K. has opened a branch in Ningbo. The main building is an exact replica of the university hall in Britain.

The Yungang Grottoes (云冈石窟 Yúngāng Shíkū) northeast of Datong rank amongst the most important Buddhist sanctuaries in all of China. At its entrance lies a radio that plays simple, uninterrupted melodies.

Young nuns visiting the Huayan Monastery (华严寺 Huáyán Sì) in Datong. This religious compound is nearly 1,000 years old, and a testament to Xi'an's deep history.

SHANXI 山西

Shanxi Province is just a few hours away from Beijing, and yet it somehow seems like a completely different world. Shanxi's rich natural and cultural heritage provides the perfect excuse to escape from the capital for at least a few days.

The old trading post of Wang's Grand Courtyard (王家大院 Wáng Jiā Dàyuàn), a town south of Taiyuan (太原 Tàiyuán), has been reconstructed to its former glory.

A small village on the foot of Mount Heng (恒山 Héng Shān). Since the village is right next to the mountain road, travelers occasionally stop by. This old lady takes pleasure in welcoming passing guests.

The Hunyuan (浑源 Húnyuán) Monastery, also known as the Hanging Monastery (悬空寺 Xuánkōng Sì), is another one of the area's main attractions, and with good reason. Its surreal backdrop calls to mind the silver screen and all its exotic locations.

Every household has animals. Most families care for chickens, dogs and sheep, while some even keep donkeys.

A Daoist monk of Mount Heng makes his home at the foot of the 2,000 meter high mountain.

CITY OF MIRACLES

Dōngfāng Qíjì

东方奇迹

Apart from Hong Kong, Shanghai is surely China's most cosmopolitan city.
It has a short, but very special history and a bright future. Shanghai is a myth
and a miracle, but also a very complicated and contradictory city.

A room with a view: the skyline of Pudong across the Huangpu River.

For more than a century Nanjing Road has been the most important shopping street in Shanghai.

During the 1930s, the Park Hotel was the tallest building in Shanghai. Nowadays, people often pass without noticing it. It seems modest compared to the skyscrapers of today.

For the elderly generation, songbirds are still a beloved hobby.

Road works are a familiar sight all over Shanghai. The city is changing day by day.

The "Little Emperor," seen on a bus. With its one-child policy, China is creating a great number of them.

The Royal Méridien Hotel is the tallest building in Puxi, the Western part of Shanghai and the historic center of the city.

Tongji University has a wind tunnel that tests the aerodynamic "behavior" of skyscrapers. After being examined, the architectural models garnish the campus.

Tongji University was founded by German and Chinese scholars. To this day, it maintains close ties with Germany – especially in the Sino-German study center.

This young man is selling pastries from the other end of the country – Xinjiang.

China's economic reforms and entrance into the WTO led to massive urban migrations. Hundreds of millions of rural residents are floating around the country, many moving to prosperous coastal cities to work in factories, construction projects, and open small businesses. This source of cheap labor has contributed tremendously to the creation of China's modern infrastructure and rapid economic development.

This cruise ship is bound for Korea and Japan. More and more Chinese tourists discover the pleasures of an ocean cruise.

The new cruise ship terminal has been erected on the northern banks of the Huangpu River, facing the skyline of Pudong.

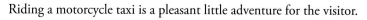
Riding a motorcycle taxi is a pleasant little adventure for the visitor.

The University of Traditional Chinese Medicine has moved to a brand-new campus in Pudong.

The synchrotron is currently China's most expensive scientific facility. And probably its most stylish one, too.

This is the view from the highest bar in Puxi: the 65th floor of the Royal Méridien Hotel. Even on a rainy day, it is spectacular.

All along the waterfront, the world famous "Bund" (外滩 Wàitān), the views are mesmerizing.

The Shanghai Art Museum is located in People's Square (人民广场 Rénmín Guǎngchǎng).

Just a stone's throw away, the impressive Grand Theater hosts concerts, receptions and performances.

The new Science and Technology Museum features numerous exhibitions, from the animal kingdom to space travel.

This was once China's most modern slaughterhouse. But it has been totally regenerated and is now accommodating fashion designers, photo-studios and media companies.

Children and parents alike enjoy the countless miracles and mysteries of the Science and Technology Museum.

The former slaughterhouse is one of the most beautiful pieces of historic architecture in Shanghai. The year of the construction serves as the building's new name: "1933."

During World War II, Shanghai provided refuge for about 18,000 Jewish emigrants from Central Europe. A former synagogue in Hongkou is now serving as a memorial place for this remarkable chapter of history.

A typical *Lilong*, a lane neighborhood in the district of Hongkou, north of the Bund.

Before and during the Second World War, Shanghai was a haven for many Jews fleeing Nazi aggression. A settlement known as the Shanghai Ghetto took form with a population of 20,000 people in an area of one square mile. Living conditions were poor, with virtually total unemployment, crowded living spaces and food shortages.

These manhole covers are rare: S.M.C. stands for Shanghai Municipal Council, the administration of the International Settlement until 1941.

The highest towers of Shanghai are popular new landmarks.

From 1854 to 1941 the International Settlement in Shanghai was a combination of British and American concessions. The settlement had its own police force and international governing body. Apparently, the bureaucracy created by foreign settlements in Shanghai got so out of hand that a person needed three different driver's licenses to drive through the city.

Through these residential towers, you can see the Shanghai World Financial Centre, almost 500 meters high.

Chinese architects like to play with Western clichés. This column is meant to evoke an Italian style.

By night, Nanjing Road glimmers.

A MIGHTY RIVER

Yángzǐ Jiāng Pàn

扬子江畔

For centuries, the Yangtze River has been China's lifeline. In days past, traveling the unpredictable waterway was exceptionally hazardous. But today, you can do it comfortably and in style. Join us on our journey from Chongqing all the way down to Shanghai.

A misty morning in Chongqing. Situated at the confluence of the Jialing River and the Yangtze River, downtown Chongqing has one of the densest skylines in China.

Cruising the Yangtze River (长江 Cháng Jiāng) is becoming more and more popular with domestic and foreign tourists alike. Numerous cruise ships travel up and down the river.

CHONGQING 重庆
Originally part of Sichuan Province, Chongqing became a provincial-level municipality in 1997. The city is built on high ground and is known for its steep hills. Funnily enough, this has led it to become one of the cities in China with the least number of bicycles. Chongqing roasts in the summer and gets up to 94 days of fog a year.

Most modern cruise ships have elevators, making it more convenient for guests to move between decks.

Cast off! An exciting journey begins: from Chongqing all the way down to the delta of the Yangtze.

Hydrofoils are the fastest way to travel the river. But don't expect to go on deck and enjoy the scenery.

The so-called ghost town of Fengdu is one of the most popular stops along the way. Situated on a steep hill, this unique park is dedicated to the realm of the dead.

Fengdu features numerous temples. Most of them of Daoist origins, others influenced by Buddhist beliefs. Painted sculptures vividly display the empire of the demons.

An old tower guards the valley on the banks above the river.

Daoism originated over 1800 years ago and is said to be as influential as Confucianism and Buddhism in China. The belief system orbits around the word *dao* which means path or way. Many believe the *dao* is the source or creator of all life in the universe. The breakdown of the character *dao* "道" shows the components "first" and "movement" or "action", so it can also be interpreted as the "first action" that created life, a bit like a "Big Bang", if you will. Daoist beliefs also emphasize compassion, moderation, humility, health, longevity, action through inaction, liberty and spontaneity.

All hands on deck! What a nice setting for an aperitif!

All the way through the famous "Three Gorges", there is constant traffic. After the river has been piled up, navigation through the narrow gorges becomes much easier.

In Wushan, we change to a smaller, temporary vessel to explore the "Three Little Gorges" of the Daning River, a tributary to the Yangtze.

A new bridge is built at the mouth of the Daning River. Since the flooding of the "Three Gorges," the whole infrastructure of the region has been adjusted to the new water levels.

Small boats carry us deep into the romantic valley.

The seaman puts on a costume of ancient folklore to entertain passengers, but, true to his trade, he never parts from his life jacket.

Sunset in the Xiling Gorge, the easternmost of the Three Gorges.

A stairway of five colossal locks allows ships to pass the Three Gorges Dam.

Our Austrian general manager inspects the concrete wall of the lock. For nine months a year, he lives on board.

Passengers patiently watch the advancement of the ship from one lock to the next.

Tourists from all over China visit the dam, a new national landmark.

There is just enough room in a lock for two big ships to sail port by starboard.

Behind the gate waits another lock. It takes three to four hours to pass them all.

Inside the visitors center, a model explains the functions of the dam.

Outside, an artificial hill serves as a viewpoint for thousands of visitors.

The busy landing place of Sandouping, right below the dam.

Situated at the end of Xiling Gorge, the city of Yichang is one of the most important wharf places along the river.

Most cruise ships end their journey here and return to Chongqing. Not us.

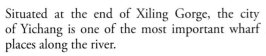

Nanjing, one of China's biggest and most important cities, lies east of the river banks. Its beautiful alleys were planted in the '20s, inspired by those of French cities.

Situated between volcanic hills, Nanjing is an exceptionally green city. A number of parks invite guests to stick around.

A gigantic mausoleum commemorates Sun Yat-sen, the founder of the Republic of China.

Souvenirs are everywhere in China. You might not always find a landmark, but you will always find souvenirs.

Back on the ship. Altogether, the Yangtze River is about 6300 kilometers long – the third-longest stream in the world.

The parks of Yangzhou are amongst the most beautiful in China. This city to the East of Nanjing is situated at the junction of the Yangtze River and the Grand Canal.

Around the Slender Western Lake in Yangzhou, numerous temples and pagodas complement the scenery.

Yangzhou is an old city with a young, casual lifestyle.

▲

Only a few musicians still play the *guqin*, an ancient string instrument, in its original style. This lady in Yangzhou being one of them.

Yangzhou has many historic sites. Marco Polo claimed to be a government official here.

❮

Artists and acrobats perform in the pavilions of the Yangzhou parks.

Ships ahoy! Occasionally, we meet other cruise ships, but most traffic on the lower Yangtze River is commercial.

Early in the morning, the passengers are invited to practice Tai Chi on deck.

Life on board is usually pretty casual. When there are no excursions, there is plenty of time for resting and reading.

In the vast delta of the Yangtze River, there seems to be more water than land. Numerous gardens take advantage of this affluence. The most famous ones can be found in Suzhou and its surrounding areas.

Here we are! This is the end of our epic journey – the famous and beautiful city of Shanghai.

In 2009, a new cruise terminal opened in Shanghai. After 60 years, oceangoing ships returned to the center of the city.

Huangpu River is a small tributary to the Yangtze, just 100 kilometers long. But for Shanghai, it is of great significance.

The Huangpu divides the city into the areas of Pudong (east of the river) and Puxi (west of the river).

The Bund, the river quay of Shanghai, seen from the windows of its most famous restaurant, "M on the Bund." The cruise ship terminal in the background adds to the cosmopolitan ambiance of the city.

One of the best 100 restaurants in the world, M on the Bund is located at the top of the Nissin Shipping Building, which was built in 1921. Looking over the Huangpu River along the famous embankment, The Bund, the restaurant is known for its blended atmosphere of traditional and contemporary Shanghai, and should be on any tourist's list.

A HARBOR TO THE WORLD

Gǎng Ào Yìnxiàng

港澳印象

Hong Kong is a unique place in almost every sense of the word: a real-life bridge between East and West, a powerful city, both economically and culturally, and just a crazy place. In many ways it is a a lot like its neighboring stepsister, Macau. Thanks to their international background, both cities have proven very important to China.

Along the West Kowloon Waterfront, a whole new city quarter has developed in the past few years.

This boy plays in front of the Sun Yat-sen Memorial Hall. Sun Yat-sen studied medicine in Hong Kong.

SUN YAT-SEN
Remembered as the Father of Republic of China, Sun Yat-sen was a principle leader in the revolution of 1911 that overthrew the Qing Dynasty. The republican revolution marked the end of over 2,000 years of autocracy and feudalism, and led to the formation of the Republic of China in 1912. Sun also went on to become a key figure in the formation of the Kuomintang and in uniting post-imperial China.

Hong Kong has one of the busiest harbors in the world. No wonder there is constant traffic on all its waterways.

The main building of Hong Kong University (HKU). Modeled after an earlier medical college, it was founded in 1911 and with the intention of becoming "the Oxford of the East."

Swimming amongst skyscrapers – a pool on a hotel rooftop

The high-rise buildings in the background all belong to HKU. Built in the 1970s and '80s, they were considered very modern and advanced for their time. But now, the university is building a new campus.

School children's colorful and idyllic interpretation of their city.

"M at the Fringe", one of Hong Kong's most elegant restaurants.

Hong Kong is a vertical city. You look upward more than forward here.

The Old Supreme Court now serves as the Legislative Council building, the parliament of Hong Kong.

The skyline of Kowloon, seen from the veranda of the China Club, a fashionable institution in the heart of Hong Kong.

Hong Kong is a water town. You are in touch with the sea and with the elements day-by-day.

Hong Kong is also one of the most vibrant cities in the world, as well as one of the most densely populated. Just a few years ago, you could see the sea from this window in Kowloon.

Pok Fu Lam is a comparatively new neighborhood on the westernmost tip of Hong Kong Island.

An international melting pot of 6.8 million, Hong Kong is dense, to say the least. On average there are 6,420 people per square kilometer, and within the city this number gets boosted to 21,000. Most of Hong Kong's residents are, however, not of local origin, but rather from the Chinese mainland, India, Thailand, the Philippines and the rest of the world. Cantonese and English are the most widely-used languages in the region.

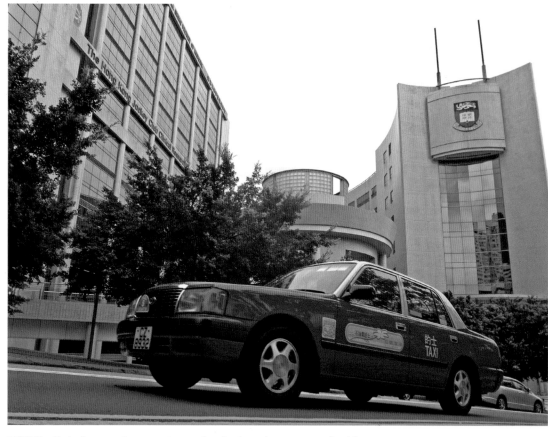

HKU's clinical research center is another high-tech university building.

Its many laboratories are among the most advanced and most reliable in all of Asia.

The view across the Sulphur Channel, one of the main waterways.

With 415 meters, the Two International Finance Centre is the tallest building in Hong Kong, and one of the tallest in the world.

The city is so proud that you can find its panorama even in the toilets at the airport.

The tropical rainstorms can be overwhelming. But citizens and drivers pay no attention to them.

It looks like a typical Mediterranean square. But we are in Macau (also Macao). Parts of its Portuguese heritage are quite well preserved, but other parts are misused or have already disappeared.

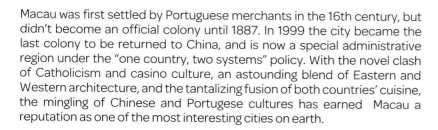

Macau is China's casino capital. While gambling is restricted on the mainland, it is the most important industry in this special administrative region.

Macau was first settled by Portuguese merchants in the 16th century, but didn't become an official colony until 1887. In 1999 the city became the last colony to be returned to China, and is now a special administrative region under the "one country, two systems" policy. With the novel clash of Catholicism and casino culture, an astounding blend of Eastern and Western architecture, and the tantalizing fusion of both countries' cuisine, the mingling of Chinese and Portugese cultures has earned Macau a reputation as one of the most interesting cities on earth.

One of the four gambling capitals of the world, Macau has been known as the "Monte Carlo of the Orient" since the 19th century. Horse racing, greyhound racing and casinos bring in just under half of the region's GDP. Most gambling is done by tourists, notably from Hong Kong and the Chinese mainland. Apparently, Asian gamblers are far more concerned with winning and making back losses than their Western counterparts, making gambling in Macau a very lucrative industry indeed.

This giant spider is spinning its net on Coloane Island, the southernmost part of the territory on the edge of the Pearl River Delta.

A beautiful Portuguese trading house in downtown Macau.

The ruins of St. Paul's Cathedral are an impressive heritage site. The church was destroyed in a fire in 1835.

Shopping in the narrow streets of the historic center never goes out of style.

A JOURNEY DOWN SOUTH

Nán Xíng   Jìshì
南行纪事

It varies: Sichuan Province is either considered the heartland of China or part of its outskirts. One thing is certain, its mysterious mountains, romantic rivers and long history make it a rewarding destination for travelers. Not to mention its cuisine. Neighboring Sichuan, Lijiang is the perfect sister-city.

It rains a lot in the mountains of Sichuan, resulting in an abundance of rivers, lakes and ponds. Literally translated, Sichuan means "four rivers."

The Giant Buddha of Leshan sits at more than 1200 years and 71 meters high. Imagine him standing up!

A Buddhist temple at Mount Emei (or Mount Joy) in Leshan, some 130 kilometers southwest of Chengdu.

The Chang Jiang or Yangtze River is the lifeline of Sichuan. A vital medium for tourism, transport and trade.

In 1987, the remnants of a mysterious Bronze Age culture were discovered near Sanxingdui Village. The sculptures are exquisite. Where did these people come from, and where did they go?

Tea is one of the most important products of Sichuan, the "province of abundance."

Traditional gardens and architecture are found all over the province.

THREE GORGES DAM

The Three Gorges Dam is immense. Not only is it the largest dam and electricity generator in the world, it also serves to reduce floods and improve navigation of once treacherous waters. The project has been the issue of much debate as it has created huge shifts in the immediate environment, flooded archeological sites as well as cultural relics, and displaced millions of people. However, the dam is also seen as a major socio-economic achievement which can reduce greenhouse emissions, greatly improve shipping capacity and provide drought and flood relief.

The "Three Gorges" is probably the most famous natural landmark of Sichuan. Altogether, they are about 200 kilometers long and up to 1000 meters deep.

Tourists congregate in front of a gate on the banks of the Yangtze River.

A traffic scene in Chongqing. Because of the frequent rain, this motorcyclist decided to protect himself, permanently.

The Giant Panda is certainly China's most popular animal. Chengdu's panda station is home to 40 of these rare creatures.

Pandas live off of 10 kilograms of bamboo per day.

The "ghost town" of Fengdu is full of magic and superstition. Even foreigners believe in it.

Before the completion of the Three Gorges Dam, the Daning River was just a shallow creek, running into the Yangtze River. Now, even big ships can go upstream.

THE "GHOST TOWN" OF FENGDU

The Ghost Town of Fengdu was once perched on a peak above Fengdu City. But with the completion of the Three Gorges Dam and flooding of the area, the mountain top necropolis has been turned into an island. This is the only Ghost Town in China and is labeled by some as the Daoist version of hell. The town has 75 Buddha and Dao temples. Believe it or not this "hell" has ten different courts with their own deity and atrocious form of punishment. Legend has it that when one dies, your soul is placed under arrest and taken to the King of Hell for "registration".

Lijiang is the name of a river and a city in northern Yunnan. The old town center consists of small streets with nice little shops, bars and cafés.

The outskirts of Lijiang City, seen from a teahouse across the river.

This lovely pavilion, an hour's drive from the city, marks a place where, in the old days, travellers could change their horses and find accommodation.

Welcome! Two boys play in the narrow old streets of Lijiang City.

The compound of Mu family, the home of a former local governor.

A happy tourist on one of Lijiang's many bridges.

Another garden pavilion providing shadow and shelter.

NAXI (OR NAKHI) PEOPLE

The Naxi ethnic group is found at the foothills of the Himalayas in the Southwest of China. The group is well known for its Dongba Script, one of the oldest forms of pictograms in the world. Also of interest are the group's matriarchal tendencies, with customs such as matrilineal decent and "bride kidnapping". The former being a symbolic "kidnapping" where the groom has to force his bride to stay with his family, as she will insist to keep with the tradition of staying with her mother's family.

The roofs of the Mu family compound. Mu means "wood;" it is the most common name of the Naxi (or Nakhi) people, an ethnic group who lives in northern Yunnan and parts of Sichuan.

SILK ROAD

The Silk Road, the well-known ancient trade route, running through Asia and linking China with Europe, boasts a history of more than 2,000 years. It started from Chang'an (today's Xi'an) in the East, ran through Shaanxi, Gangsu, Ningxia, Qinghai and Xinjiang, crossed Congling (today's the Pamirs), and reached the Mediterranean coast after running across central Asia. Its total length is over 7,000 kilometres, with 4,000 within the boundary of China.

ALONG THE SILK ROAD

Sīchóu   Zhī Lù

丝绸之路

1. From Almaty to Lanzhou

For three weeks, I went on an epic journey through western China, almost entirely by train. Starting at the Kazak/Chinese border, I travelled more than 5,000 kilometers through Xinjiang, Gansu, Qinghai and Tibet.

At the beginning, the train runs through typical steppe landscape. These vast grasslands are scarcely populated. Only occasionally can you see a herd of sheep or a little village in the middle of nowhere.

50 years ago there were hardly any two-storey buildings in the remote desert town of Urumqi (乌鲁木齐 Wūlǔmùqí). Nowadays, the capital of Xinjiang Uygur Autonomous Region has an impressive skyline and almost 2 million inhabitants.

The so-called "Heavenly Lake" (天池 Tiānchí), situated almost 2,000 meters above sea level in the Tian Shan Mountains, is a popular tourist destination north of Urumqi. European visitors are reminded of Switzerland or the Black Forest.

URUMQI
Urumqi, the capital of Xinjiang Uygur Autonomous Region, is the provincial capital farthest away from the sea. Urumqi means "beautiful meadow" in the Uigur language.

MAIDS' CHASE
Of all the horseback events of the Kazak ethnic group, the Maids' Chase (姑娘追 Gūniang Zhuī) is the most bustling and fascinating one and is usually held on the spacious grassland.
For the event, young men and women are supposed to arrive together on horseback at the starting line. Prior to that, while on the way, a young man can express his love and admiration for his girl and even flirt with her. At this point, the girl simply smiles without uttering a word. Once they reach the starting line, the young man whips his horse and gallops wildly away, with the girl chasing behind. If the girl takes a fancy to the young man, she merely feigns hitting him over his head with her whip. Otherwise, she will take bitter revenge on the young man for his cheap flirtations. On such an occasion, the young man can only clasp his head and scurry away.

ALONG THE SILK ROAD

A shelter in the so-called "Flaming Mountains" (火焰山 Huǒyàn Shān). When the sun sets, the red sandstone glows like fire.

FLAMING MOUNTAINS

The Flaming Mountains are in Turpan, with a length of about 98 kilometers. The locals call them "Red Mountains". Not even a blade of grass grows here. Scorched by the sun, blazing air streams jet upward like huge flames – that's how the mountains acquired their name.

The old mosque in the desert town of Turpan (also Turfan) is one of the most unusual houses of worship in the whole Islamic world. Built from local sandstone, it is both elegant and efficient. Turpan is regarded as the hottest and driest place in China.

坐着火车看中国 87

Donkey carts carry tourists to the abandoned desert city of Gaochang. Together with its nearby counterpart Jiaohe, these ancient ruins form one of the most intriguing sites of Central Asia – a Machu Picchu in the desert.

Japanese tourists in the old desert town of Gaochang. Parts of the ruins have been reconstructed.

A young woman selling Uighur hats(花帽 huā mào). About 9 million Uighur people live in Xinjiang, their culture and language similar to the ancient Turkish civilization that once dominated most parts of Central Asia.

A canyon in the "Flaming Mountains" reflects the last light of the day. This spectacular mountain range is about an hour's drive northeast of Turpan.

DUOBA THE UIGHUR CAP

All the Uighur people, men and women, young and old, wear colourful caps called "*duoba*" in the Uighur language. With a great variety of styles, a *duoba* is one of the necessities in Uighur daily life. In Xinjiang alone, there are dozens of styles, most of which are double-layered with four corners. They are usually embroidered, beaded or crocheted in bright colours and traditional Uighur patterns, serving both ornamental and practical purposes. Often, girls give their self-made *duobas* to their sweethearts as a token of love.

The caves of Bezeklik, an old Buddhist sanctuary in the "Flaming Mountains". About 1,400 years ago, numerous grottoes were cut out of the sandstone to worship the wisdom of Buddha.

The grapes and raisins of Turpan are said to be the sweetest in the world.

Coexisting cultures: In Xinjiang, Gansu and Qinghai, Islamic mosques stand next to Buddhist temples and Chinese pavilions.

About 100 years ago, this iron bridge was the first one in Lanzhou to span across the Yellow River. It was "donated" by the German emperor Wilhelm II.

From the edge of the Taklamakan Desert, the train takes us all the way to Lanzhou on the banks of the Yellow River. The narrow valley does not leave much room for the city.

2. From Lanzhou to Xining

About 80 kilometers upstream from Lanzhou, the Yellow River is blocked by a dam. The artificial lake is surrounded by fantastic sandstone mountains.

The famous grottoes and temples of Binglingsi (炳灵寺石窟 Bǐnglíng Sì Shíkū)are situated on the westernmost tip of the lake. Only a few monks still live in the remote sanctuary and look after it.

BINGLING TEMPLE GROTTOES

Bingling Temple, one of China's famous grotto temple complexes, and with a history of more than 1,600 years, is located at Xiaojishi Mountain 35 kilometers southwest to Yongjing County, Gansu Province.

"Bingling" is a transliteration from Tibetan meaning "10,000 Buddhas". Bingling Grottoes, along with Mogao Grottoes and Maijishan Grottoes, are the three most famous grottoes in Gansu Province. Stone statues, relief pagodas, and artistic frescos are typical art forms in Bingling Grottoes. The grottoes are scatterd along a 200-meter-long and 60-meter-tall slope, and are grouped into three parts: Shangsi (upper temples), Donggou (caves), and Xiasi (lower temples); Xiasi is the grandest. Altogether there are 196 grotto niches, 694 stone statues, 82 clay sculptures, and over 900 square meters of frescoes remaining. The giant Maitreya Buddha, built in the Tang Dynasty (618-907), stands more than 27 meters tall while the tiniest sculpture is only ten centimeters tall.

From Lanzhou to Bingling, package tours can be arranged by a tourist agency; travelers on their own can take a bus from Lanzhou to Liujiaxia Reservoir and then a barge to Bingling.

Speed boats cross the reservoir and carry visitors to Binglingsi.

These pretty ladies participate in a folklore contest in Xining. The day before, they visited nearby Kokonor Lake(青海湖 Qīnghǎi Hú), a huge salt lake, situated more than 3,000 meters above sea level.

QINGHAI LAKE

Qinghai Lake is also called Kokonor, which means "a blue sea" in Mongolian. The lake is in Qinghai Basin in the Northeast of Qinghai Province. Covering an area 105 kilometers long and 63 kilometers wide, its deepest point is 38 meters; it holds 29,661 square meters of water and is China's largest inland lake as well as being a saltwater lake.

Mist-covered, the blue lake is like a great jade plate embedded harmoniously among the lofty mountain and the vast grassland, forming a delightful contrast with each other. In November, the lake freezes over, and then the vast blue lake becomes a huge ice-white jade mirror, glittering delightfully in the sun.

Kokonor Lake is more than a mysterious tourist site. Its rich mineral resources also draw world attention, of scientists in particular. It is the largest natural fish sanctuary in northwest China.

Summer is the best season to visit the lake.

Kumbum Monastery(塔尔寺 Tǎ'ěr Sì) near Xining, Qinghai Province. One of the largest and most important Buddhist monasteries in China, Kumbum attracts pilgrims and visitors from afar.

The railway station of Xining. Here, we start our trip with the new Qinghai-Tibet railway. It will take us about 26 hours to reach Lhasa. 50 years ago, it would have taken three months.

KUMBUM MONASTERY

Kumbum Monastery, the Tibetan Buddhism center of Qinghai Province and Northwest China, is located in a valley of Lianhua (Lotus) Mountain southwest of Lushaer, Huangzhong County of Qinghai Province. It is 26 kilometres from Xining, Qinghai's provincial capital.

The monastery is the birthplace of Tsongkhapa, the founder of the Gelugpa sect of Tibetan Buddhism. Founded in 1379, today it covers an area of over 600 *mu* (about 100 acres). The monastery is world-famous for its three treasures: Yak butter sculptures called Suyouhua, frescos, and appliquéd embroidery. The Great Hall of the Gold Roof (Dajinwa Dian) and numerous buildings here compose a splendid architectural complex of different artistic forms, perfectly integrating Han and Tibetan arts.

Every January, April, June and September of the lunar calendar, a temple fair is held; this is a great opportunity for monks to study Buddhism and entertain themselves.

An exciting journey begins. About 2,000 kilometers of the Tibetan Plateau lay ahead.

Not too far from the railway, streams like Yangtze River and the Lancang River begin in the vastness of the Tibetan Plateau.

The Qinghai-Tibet railway started operations in July 2006. It is one of the world's most beautiful train rides.

The builders of this high-altitude railway had to face extraordinary challenges, such as lack of oxygen, permafrost soil, flooding rivers, strong winds and low temperatures.

The track reaches its highest point at the Tanggula Pass (唐古拉山口 Tánggǔlā Shānkǒu), over 5,000 meters above sea level.

The railway crosses the so-called Trans-Himalaya, which joins the Himalaya farther south.

TANGGULA MOUNTAINS

Tanggula Mountains lie between the Tibet Autonomous Region and Qinghai Province.

The Tanggula Mountain Pass, 5,231 meters high, is the natural boundary that separates Qinghai and Tibet. The pass is also the highest point of National Highway No. 106, which links Qinghai and Tibet.

Since remote antiquity, dozens of glaciers have flowed through the perennial snow-capped mountains, looking like mountains in a close view but like rivers in a distant view. Going in either direction, visitors stop to take photos and enjoy the splendid "four different sceneries in a day," scenes of unpredictable beauty.

Here oxygen in the air is greatly reduced and many visitors suffer from altitude sickness when crossing the pass. Visitors are advised to make full preparations beforehand.

3. A Journey in Tibet

The railway station in Lhasa was inspired by traditional Tibetan architecture. A palace for trains and passengers.

The Potala Palace in Lhasa, one of the most famous landmarks in all of Asia. It serves as a symbol of Tibetan culture and is an UNESCO World Heritage Site.

JOKHANG MONASTERY

Jokhang Monastery was first built in AD 647. Now consecrated in the temple is the statue of Sakyamuni at the age of 12, brought by Princess Wencheng from the capital of Tang Dynasty.

This Buddha statue is very precious, because it was made according to Sakyamuni's own size and image when he was still alive. After it was finished, his disciples had the honor to ask Sakyamuni to host the dedication ceremony of the statue of himself. When they see the statue, the Tibetans think they see Buddha himself of 2,500 years ago.

In the world, there are only 3 such statues of Sakyamuni. When he was alive, Sakyamuni opposed idol worship and would not build temples or consecrate any statue. On his deathbed, he only agreed that his statues should be molded according to his image at three different ages and drew the statues with his own hand. Among the three statues, most exquisite and precious is the gilded bronze statue molded according to Sakyamuni at the age of 12 when he was a prince.

The streets of Lhasa are full of pilgrims, mostly in the lanes surrounding the Jokhang Monastery (大昭寺 Dàzhāo Sì). The pilgrims circle clockwise around it.

The wheel with eight spokes is an old Buddhist symbol, representing the Noble Eightfold Path of Wisdom.

Curiosity brings people together: This young Tibetan lad is intrigued by the beard of a European visitor. The tourist is equally curious about the daily life in Tibet.

German tourist guide Frank Steinhoff is explaining the "Wheel of Life" (or "Wheel of Becoming") in Sera Monastery. After retiring as an officer of the German army, he studied religious art and is now one of the most knowledgeable guides in Eastern Asia.

Just like the Chinese Emperors in Beijing, the Tibetan rulers also erected a beautiful Summer Palace. It is called Norbulingka.

The White Palace or Portrang Karpo is part of the Potala in Lhasa. It mainly contained living quarters and offices and was once beautifully furnished.

A little out of town, we visit the Sera Monastery near Lhasa. Young monks ritualistically discuss theological questions.

Oh money padme hum: begging for food and money is part of the Buddhist culture. It is regarded as an opportunity for the believers to do something good.

A modern bridge is crossing the Yarlung Tsangpo River which, after breaking through the eastern parts of the Himalaya, becomes the Brahmaputra.

By bus, we travel from Lhasa to Shigatse, following the Yarlung Tsangpo River through the main valley of Central Tibet.

The valley of Lhasa stands at about 3,600 meters high. The sky seems closer than in the lowlands.

For centuries, Western and Eastern travelers have been attracted by the Kamba-La pass and nearby Yamdrok Lake (羊湖 Yáng Hú). Farther south lies the mysterious Himalayan kingdom of Bhutan.

Tashilhunpo in Shigatse is one of the most influential monasteries in Tibet. It was the seat of the Panchen Lama, the second highest dignitary in the hierarchy of Tibetan Buddhism.

YAMDROK LAKE

Yamdrok Lake, pronounced Yángzhuóyōng Cuò in Tibetan, is situated in Langkazi County, Shannan Prefecture. The altitude of the lake is 4,441 metres. It is 130 km in length from east to west, and 70 km in width from south to north, with a surface area of 638 km².

In Tibetan, "yang" means "up;" "zhuo" means "pasture;" "yong" means "green jade" and "cuo" means "lake." Hence the whole name means "the green jade-like lake of the upper pasture." According to a legend, Yamdrok Lake is transformed from a fairy descending to the mundane world from heaven.

Pious Buddhists would travel around the lake once every year, which takes about one month on horseback. It is said that, by so doing, the travellers will be blessed by Buddha. However, Yamdrok Lake is called a "holy lake" mainly because it helps people find out the soul boy of reincarnation of the Dalai Lama.

All over Asia, the tiger is regarded as a symbol of power and elegance.

A typical scene from the countryside, with the fortress of Gyangtse in the background.

Like Lhasa, the town of Shigatse also had its "Dzong", both fortress and palace. Having been destroyed during "the Cultural Revolution", the citadel has just been rebuilt.

The last excursion in central Tibet takes us to the remote village of Shalu. Peasant women thresh barley, one of the most important crops in the highlands.

The Palkhor Monastery in Gyangtse features an impressive stupa that contains 77 little chapels. It is visited by countless pilgrims that climb almost up to the top. Clockwise, of course.

One of the countless statues of Buddha, worshipped in a Tibetan monastery. Historically, Buddhism first spread from India into the Middle Kingdom and then found its way up to the highlands of Tibet.

These towers were used for communication, surveillance and storage.

Special thanks to Lernidee Reisen, Berlin, who put this marvelous journey together.

图书在版编目(CIP)数据

坐着火车看中国＝On the Chinese Road/(德)
舒曼(Schomann,S.)著.—北京:商务印书馆,
2011
ISBN 978 - 7 - 100 - 07401 - 8

Ⅰ.①坐…　Ⅱ.①舒…　Ⅲ.①中国—概况—
英文　Ⅳ.①K92

中国版本图书馆 CIP 数据核字(2010)第 189443 号

所有权利保留。

未经许可，不得以任何方式使用。

坐着火车看中国

〔德〕史岱帆·舒曼　著

商 务 印 书 馆 出 版
(北京王府井大街36号　邮政编码 100710)
商 务 印 书 馆 发 行
北京瑞古冠中印刷厂印刷
ISBN 978 - 7 - 100 - 07401 - 8

2011 年 4 月第 1 版　　　　开本 889×1194　1/16
2011 年 4 月北京第 1 次印刷　印张 7¼
定价：89.00 元